The Orchard Book of Nursery Rhymes

Daffy-down-dilly is new come to town,
With a yellow petticoat and a green gown.

The Orchard Book of
NURSERY RHYMES

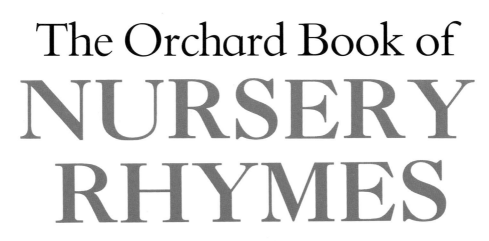

Rhymes chosen by Zena Sutherland
Pictures by Faith Jaques

Orchard Books · New York

For Julian, Robin and Stephanie
F. J.

Orchard Books
A division of Franklin Watts, Inc.
387 Park Avenue South
New York, NY 10016
Manufactured in Great Britain
10 9 8 7 6 5 4 3 2 1

Library of Congress Cataloging-in-Publication Data

Sutherland, Zena.
    The Orchard book of nursery rhymes/rhymes chosen by
Zena Sutherland; pictures by Faith Jaques. — 1st American
ed.
    p.   cm.
    Summary: The well-known authority in the field of
children's literature presents a selection of familiar nursery
rhymes.
    ISBN 0-531-05903-0
    1. Nursery rhymes. 2. Children's poetry. [1. Nursery
rhymes.]
I. Jaques, Faith, ill. II. Title.
PZ8.3.S970r 1990
398.8—dc20   89-71002
                                                        CIP
                                                        AC

Introduction

Nursery rhymes have been handed down from parent to child for centuries as part of the oral tradition. Whether songs, stories, games, ABCs, riddles, tongue-twisters, counting rhymes, fingerplays, nonsense verse, or pure poetry, the rhymes are part of the cultural heritage of every English-speaking country.

There is an immediate and irresistible appeal to the verses. They may extend beyond children's experiences, but they are almost entirely within their comprehension. The verses are perfectly suited to a young child's attention span, and often tell stories. They are lilting, bouncy, and rhythmic — a joy to listen to or recite. Many are full of sheer nonsense, but a young child delights in the idea of a cow jumping over the moon.

The verses are a perfect introduction to poetry, containing alliteration, cumulation, repetition, and rhyme. They encourage the development of a wide range of language skills, and some have the fluidity, shifting patterns of wordplay, and flashes of vivid imagery that are the touchstone of fine poetic style.

This collection contains all the best-known and well-loved verses of the English language. The illustrations place the verses in an eighteenth-century setting, reflecting the historical period when many of them first appeared in print. The rhymes offer pleasure to both parent and child, especially when shared.

Hush, little baby, don't say a word,
Papa's going to buy you a mockingbird.
If the mockingbird won't sing,
Papa's going to buy you a diamond ring.
If the diamond ring turns to brass,
Papa's going to buy you a looking glass.
If the looking glass gets broke,
Papa's going to buy you a billy goat.
If that billy goat runs away,
Papa's going to buy you another today.

Bye, baby bunting,
Daddy's gone a-hunting,
To get a little rabbit's skin
To wrap the baby bunting in.

Rock-a-bye, baby, on the treetop,
When the wind blows, the cradle will rock;
When the bough breaks, the cradle will fall,
Down will come baby, cradle, and all.

This little pig went to market,
This little pig stayed home,
This little pig had roast beef,
This little pig had none,
And this little pig cried, Wee-wee-wee,
All the way home.

A was an apple pie.

B bit it.

C cut it.

D dealt it.

E eat it.

F fought for it.

G got it.

H had it.

I inspected it.

J jumped for it.

K kept it.

L longed for it.

M mourned for it.

P peeped in it.

N nodded at it.

Q quartered it.

O opened it.

R ran for it.

S stole it.

T took it.

U upset it.

V viewed it.

W wanted it.

X, Y, Z, and ampersand
All wished for a piece in hand.

Anna Elise,
She jumped with surprise;
The surprise was so quick,.
It played her a trick;
The trick was so rare,
She jumped in a chair;
The chair was so frail,
She jumped in a pail;
The pail was so wet,
She jumped in a net;
The net was so small,
She jumped on a ball;
The ball was so round,
She jumped on the ground;
And ever since then
She's been turning around.

Hey! diddle, diddle,
The cat and the fiddle,
The cow jumped over the moon.
The little dog laughed
To see such sport,
And the dish ran away with the spoon.

Pat-a-cake, pat-a-cake, baker's man,
Bake me a cake as fast as you can.
Pat it and prick it and mark it with B,
And put it in the oven for baby and me.

Cock-a-doodle-doo!
My dame has lost her shoe,
My master's lost his fiddling stick,
And knows not what to do.

One, two,
Buckle my shoe;

Three, four,
Knock at the door;

Five, six,
Pick up sticks;

Seven, eight,
Lay them straight;

Nine, ten,
A big fat hen;

Eleven, twelve,
Dig and delve;

Thirteen, fourteen,
Maids a-courting;

Fifteen, sixteen,
Maids in the kitchen;

Seventeen, eighteen,
Maids a-waiting;

Nineteen, twenty,
My plate's empty.

Boys and girls come out to play,
The moon doth shine as bright as day.
Leave your supper, and leave your sleep,
And join your playfellows in the street.
Come with a whoop, and come with a call,
Come with a good will or not at all.
Up the ladder and down the wall,
A half-penny loaf will serve us all.
You find milk, and I'll find flour,
And we'll have a pudding in half an hour.

In a cottage in Fife
Lived a man and his wife,
Who, believe me, were comical folk.
For, to people's surprise,
They both saw with their eyes,
And their tongues moved whenever they spoke.
When quite fast asleep,
I've been told that to keep
Their eyes open they could not contrive.
They walked on their feet,
And 'twas thought what they eat
Helped, with drinking, to keep them alive.

Pease porridge hot,
Pease porridge cold,
Pease porridge in the pot
Nine days old.
Some like it hot,
Some like it cold,
Some like it in the pot
Nine days old.

A diller, a dollar,
A ten o'clock scholar,
What makes you come so soon?
You used to come at ten o'clock
But now you come at noon.

Bow-wow, says the dog,
Mew, mew, says the cat,
Grunt, grunt, goes the hog,
And squeak goes the rat.
Tu-whoo, says the owl,
Caw, caw, says the crow,
Quack, quack, says the duck,
What cuckoos say you know.

Hector Protector was dressed all in green;
Hector Protector was sent to the Queen.
The Queen did not like him,
No more did the King,
So Hector Protector was sent back again.

Yankee Doodle came to town,
Riding on a pony;
He stuck a feather in his cap,
And called it macaroni.

Gregory Griggs, Gregory Griggs
Had twenty-seven different wigs.
He wore them up, he wore them down,
To please the people of the town.
He wore them east, he wore them west,
But never could tell which one he loved best.

Sing a song of sixpence,
A pocket full of rye;
Four and twenty blackbirds
Baked in a pie.

When the pie was opened,
The birds began to sing;
Wasn't that a dainty dish,
To set before the king?

The king was in his counting-house
Counting out his money;
The queen was in the parlor
Eating bread and honey.

The maid was in the garden
Hanging out the clothes,
When down came a blackbird
And snapped off her nose.

Pussycat, pussycat, where have you been?
I've been to London to look at the Queen.
Pussycat, pussycat, what did you there?
I frightened a little mouse under her chair.

Three blind mice, see how they run!
They all ran after the farmer's wife,
Who cut off their tails with the carving knife.
Did you ever see such a sight in your life,
As three blind mice?

Wee Willie Winkie runs through the town,
Upstairs and downstairs in his nightgown,
Rapping at the window, crying through the lock,
Are the children all in bed, for now it's eight o'clock?

Diddle, diddle, dumpling, my son John,
Went to bed with his trousers on;
One shoe off and one shoe on,
Diddle, diddle, dumpling, my son John.

Humpty Dumpty sat on a wall,
Humpty Dumpty had a great fall.
All the King's horses and all the King's men
Couldn't put Humpty together again.

Jack Sprat could eat no fat,
His wife could eat no lean;
And so, between them both, you see,
They licked the platter clean.

Georgie Porgie, pudding and pie,
Kissed the girls and made them cry.
When the boys came out to play,
Georgie Porgie ran away.

Peter, Peter, pumpkin eater,
Had a wife and couldn't keep her.
He put her in a pumpkin shell
And there he kept her very well.

The Queen of Hearts,
She made some tarts,
All on a summer's day.
The Knave of Hearts,
He stole those tarts,
And took them clean away.

The King of Hearts
Called for the tarts,
And beat the knave full sore.
The Knave of Hearts
Brought back the tarts,
And vowed he'd steal no more.

Little Tommy Tucker
Sings for his supper.
What shall we give him?
White bread and butter.
How shall he cut it
Without a knife?
How will he be married
Without a wife?

Little Polly Flinders
Sat among the cinders,
Warming her pretty little toes.
Her mother came and caught her,
And whipped her little daughter
For spoiling her nice new clothes.

Little Boy Blue,
Come blow your horn,
The sheep's in the meadow,
The cow's in the corn.
Where is the boy
Who looks after the sheep?
He's under a haystack
Fast asleep.
Will you wake him?
No, not I,
For, if I do,
He's sure to cry.

Little Miss Muffet
Sat on a tuffet,
Eating her curds and whey.
Along came a spider,
Who sat down beside her
And frightened Miss Muffet away.

Old King Cole
Was a merry old soul,
And a merry old soul was he.
He called for his pipe,
And he called for his bowl,
And he called for his fiddlers three.

Every fiddler he had a fine fiddle,
And a very fine fiddle had he.
Oh, there's none so rare,
As can compare,
With King Cole and his fiddlers three.

See-saw, Margery Daw,
Jacky shall have a new master.
Jacky shall have but a penny a day
Because he can't work any faster.

Mary, Mary, quite contrary,
How does your garden grow?
With silver bells and cockle shells,
And pretty maids all in a row.

Little Bo-peep has lost her sheep,
And doesn't know where to find them.
Leave them alone, and they'll come home,
Bringing their tails behind them.

Little Bo-peep fell fast asleep,
And dreamed she heard them bleating.
But when she awoke, she found it a joke,
For they were still a-fleeting.

Then up she took her little crook,
Determined for to find them.
She found them indeed, but it made her heart bleed,
For they'd left their tails behind them.

It happened one day, as Bo-peep did stray
Into a meadow hard by,
There she espied their tails side by side,
All hung on a tree to dry.

She heaved a sigh, and wiped her eye,
And over the hillocks went rambling,
And tried what she could, as a shepherdess should,
To tack again each to its lambkin.

There was an old woman who lived in a shoe,
She had so many children she didn't know what to do.
She gave them some broth without any bread;
She whipped them all soundly and put them to bed.

Simple Simon met a pieman
Going to the fair.
Says Simple Simon to the pieman,
Let me taste your ware.

Says the pieman to Simple Simon,
Show me first your penny.
Says Simple Simon to the pieman,
Indeed I have not any.

Ding, dong, bell,
Pussy's in the well!
Who put her in?
Little Johnny Green.
Who pulled her out?
Little Tommy Stout.
What a naughty boy was that
To try to drown poor pussycat,
Who never did him any harm,
And killed the mice in his father's barn.

Tom, Tom, the piper's son,
Stole a pig and away he run.
The pig was eat,
And Tom was beat,
And Tom went howling down the street.

Ring-a-ring o' roses,
A pocket full of posies,
A-tishoo! A-tishoo!
We all fall down.

The cows are in the meadow,
Lying fast asleep,
A-tishoo! A-tishoo!
We all get up again.

Jack and Jill
Went up the hill,
To fetch a pail of water.
Jack fell down,
And broke his crown,
And Jill came tumbling after.

Baa, baa, black sheep,
Have you any wool?
Yes, sir, yes, sir,
Three bags full.
One for the master,
And one for the dame,
And one for the little boy
Who lives down the lane.

Mary had a little lamb,
Its fleece was white as snow,
And everywhere that Mary went,
The lamb was sure to go.

It followed her to school one day,
That was against the rule.
It made the children laugh and play
To see a lamb at school.

And so the teacher turned it out,
But still it lingered near
And waited patiently about,
Till Mary did appear.

Why does the lamb love Mary so?
The eager children cry.
Why, Mary loves the lamb, you know,
The teacher did reply.

Bobby Shaftoe's gone to sea,
Silver buckles at his knee.
He'll come back and marry me,
Bonny Bobby Shaftoe!

Bobby Shaftoe's bright and fair,
Combing down his yellow hair.
He's my love forever more,
Bonny Bobby Shaftoe!

Polly put the kettle on,
Polly put the kettle on,
Polly put the kettle on,
We'll all have tea.

Sukey take it off again,
Sukey take it off again,
Sukey take it off again,
They've all gone away.

Goosey, goosey gander,
Whither shall I wander?
Upstairs and downstairs,
And in my lady's chamber.
There I met an old man,
Who would not say his prayers,
I took him by the left leg
And threw him down the stairs.

I had a little nut tree,
Nothing would it bear
But a silver nutmeg
And a golden pear.
The King of Spain's daughter
Came to visit me,
And all for the sake
Of my little nut tree.

Little Jack Horner
Sat in the corner,
Eating his Christmas pie.
He put in his thumb,
And pulled out a plum,
And said, What a good boy am I!

Old Mother Hubbard
Went to the cupboard,
To fetch her poor dog a bone;
But when she got there
The cupboard was bare,
And so the poor dog had none.

Hickety, pickety, my black hen,
She lays eggs for gentlemen.
Gentlemen come every day,
To see what my black hen doth lay.
Sometimes nine, and sometimes ten,
Hickety, pickety, my black hen.

Hickory, dickory, dock,
The mouse ran up the clock.
The clock struck one,
The mouse ran down,
Hickory, dickory, dock.

I saw a ship a-sailing,
A-sailing on the sea,
And oh, but it was laden
With pretty things for thee.

There were comfits in the cabin,
And apples in the hold.
The sails were made of silk,
And the masts were all of gold.

The four and twenty sailors,
That stood between the decks,
Were four and twenty white mice
With chains about their necks.

The captain was a duck
With a packet on his back,
And when the ship began to move
The captain said, Quack! Quack!

This is the house that Jack built.

This is the malt,
That lay in the house that Jack built.

This is the rat,
That ate the malt,
That lay in the house that Jack built.

This is the cat,
That killed the rat,
That ate the malt,
That lay in the house that Jack built.

This is the dog,
That worried the cat,
That killed the rat,
That ate the malt,
That lay in the house that Jack built.

This is the cow with the crumpled horn,
That tossed the dog,
That worried the cat,
That killed the rat,
That ate the malt,
That lay in the house that Jack built.

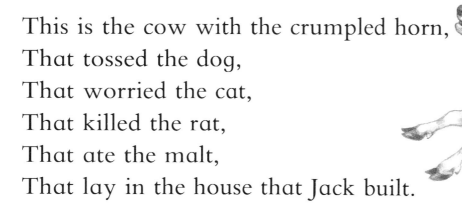

This is the maiden all forlorn,
That milked the cow with the crumpled horn,
That tossed the dog,
That worried the cat,
That killed the rat,
That ate the malt,
That lay in the house that Jack built.

This is the man all tattered and torn,
That kissed the maiden all forlorn,
That milked the cow with the crumpled horn,
That tossed the dog,
That worried the cat,
That killed the rat,
That ate the malt,
That lay in the house that Jack built.

This is the priest all shaven and shorn,
That married the man all tattered and torn,
That kissed the maiden all forlorn,
That milked the cow with the crumpled horn,
That tossed the dog,
That worried the cat,
That killed the rat,
That ate the malt,
That lay in the house that Jack built.

This is the cock that crowed in the morn,
That waked the priest all shaven and shorn,
That married the man all tattered and torn,
That kissed the maiden all forlorn,
That milked the cow with the crumpled horn,
That tossed the dog,
That worried the cat,
That killed the rat,
That ate the malt,
That lay in the house that Jack built.

This is the farmer sowing his corn,
That kept the cock that crowed in the morn,
That waked the priest all shaven and shorn,
That married the man all tattered and torn,
That kissed the maiden all forlorn,
That milked the cow with the crumpled horn,
That tossed the dog,
That worried the cat,
That killed the rat,
That ate the malt,
That lay in the house that Jack built.

Three little kittens, they lost their mittens,
And they began to cry,
Oh, mother dear, we sadly fear
Our mittens we have lost.
What! lost your mittens, you naughty kittens!
Then you shall have no pie.
Mee-ow, mee-ow, mee-ow,
No, you shall have no pie.

The three little kittens, they found their mittens,
And they began to cry,
Oh, mother dear, see here, see here,
Our mittens we have found.
Put on your mittens, you silly kittens,
And you shall have some pie.
Purr-r, purr-r, purr-r,
Oh, let us have some pie.

The three little kittens put on their mittens,
And soon ate up the pie.
Oh, mother dear, we greatly fear
Our mittens we have soiled.
What! soiled your mittens, you naughty kittens!
Then they began to sigh.
Mee-ow, mee-ow, mee-ow,
Then they began to sigh.

The three little kittens they washed their mittens.
And hung them out to dry.
Oh! mother dear, look here, look here,
Our mittens we have washed.
What! washed your mittens, then you're good kittens,
But I smell a rat close by.
Mee-ow, mee-ow, mee-ow,
We smell a rat close by.

Higglety, pigglety, pop!
The dog has eaten the mop;
The pig's in a hurry,
The cat's in a flurry,
Higglety, pigglety, pop!

There was a maid on Scrabble Hill,
And if not dead, she lives there still.
She grew so tall, she reached the sky,
And on the moon hung clothes to dry.

Three young rats with black felt hats,
Three young ducks with white straw flats,
Three young dogs with curling tails,
Three young cats with demi-veils,
Went out to walk with three young pigs
In satin vests and sorrel wigs.
But suddenly it chanced to rain,
And so they all went home again.

I do not like thee, Doctor Fell,
The reason why I cannot tell.
But this I know, and know full well,
I do not like thee, Doctor Fell.

There was a young farmer of Leeds,
Who swallowed six packets of seeds.
It soon came to pass
He was covered with grass,
And he couldn't sit down for the weeds.

Doctor Foster went to Gloucester
In a shower of rain.
He stepped in a puddle,
Right up to his middle,
And never went there again.

Peter Piper picked a peck of pickled peppers;
A peck of pickled peppers Peter Piper picked.
If Peter Piper picked a peck of pickled peppers,
Where's the peck of pickled peppers Peter Piper picked?

How much wood would a woodchuck chuck,
If a woodchuck could chuck wood?
He would chuck as much wood
As a woodchuck could,
If a woodchuck could chuck wood.

Moses supposes his toeses are roses,
But Moses supposes erroneously,
For nobody's toeses are posies of roses,
As Moses supposes his toeses to be.

Betty Botter bought some butter,
But, she said, the butter's bitter;
If I put it in my batter
It will make my batter bitter.
But a bit of better butter,
Will make my batter better.
So she bought a bit of butter,
Better than her bitter butter,
And she put it in her batter
And the batter was not bitter.
So 'twas better Betty Botter
Bought a bit of better butter.

Monday's child is
fair of face,

Tuesday's child is
full of grace,

Wednesday's child is
full of woe,

Thursday's child has
far to go,

Friday's child is
loving and giving,

Saturday's child works
hard for a living,

But the child that's born on the Sabbath day
Is bonny and blithe and good and gay.

Jack be nimble,
Jack be quick,
Jack jump over
The candlestick.

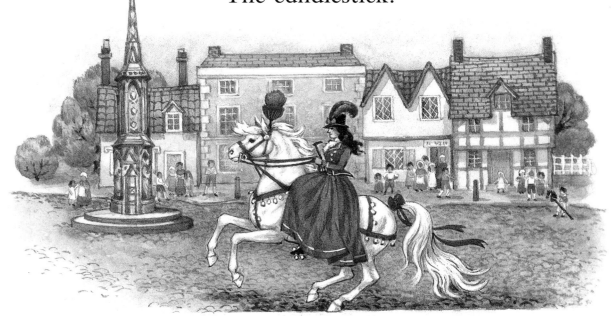

Ride a cock-horse to Banbury Cross,
To see a fine lady upon a white horse.
Rings on her fingers and bells on her toes,
She shall have music wherever she goes.

There was a crooked man
And he walked a crooked mile,
He found a crooked sixpence
Against a crooked stile.
He bought a crooked cat,
Which caught a crooked mouse,
And they all lived together
In a little crooked house.

One misty, moisty morning,
When cloudy was the weather,
I chanced to meet an old man,
Clothed all in leather.

He began to compliment
And I began to grin,
How do you do, and how do you do,
And how do you do again?

Flying-man, Flying-man,
Up in the sky,
Where are you going to,
Flying so high?

Over the mountains
And over the sea,
Flying-man, Flying-man,
Can't you take me?

There was an old woman tossed up in a basket,
Seventeen times as high as the moon.
Where she was going I couldn't but ask it,
For in her hand she carried a broom.

Old woman, old woman, old woman, quoth I,
Where are you going to up so high?
To brush the cobwebs off the sky!
May I go with you? Aye, by and by.

Here we go round the mulberry bush,
The mulberry bush, the mulberry bush.
Here we go round the mulberry bush,
On a cold and frosty morning.

This is the way we wash our hands,
Wash our hands, wash our hands.
This is the way we wash our hands,
On a cold and frosty morning.

This is the way we wash our clothes,
Wash our clothes, wash our clothes.
This is the way we wash our clothes,
On a cold and frosty morning.

This is the way we go to school,
Go to school, go to school.
This is the way we go to school,
On a cold and frosty morning.

This is the way we come out of school,
Come out of school, come out of school.
This is the way we come out of school,
On a cold and frosty morning.

The north wind doth blow,
And we shall have snow,
And what will poor Robin do then?
Poor thing!
He'll sit in a barn,
And keep himself warm,
And hide his head under his wing.
Poor thing!

Christmas is coming,
The geese are getting fat,
Please to put a penny
In the old man's hat.
If you haven't got a penny,
A ha'penny will do.
If you haven't got a ha'penny,
Then God bless you!

The first day of Christmas,
My true love sent to me,
A partridge in a pear tree.

The second day of Christmas,
My true love sent to me,
Two turtle doves, and
A partridge in a pear tree.

The third day of Christmas,
My true love sent to me,
Three French hens,
Two turtle doves, and
A partridge in a pear tree.

74

The fourth day of Christmas,
My true love sent to me,
Four colly birds,
Three French hens,
Two turtle doves, and
A partridge in a pear tree.

The fifth day of Christmas,
My true love sent to me,
Five gold rings,
Four colly birds,
Three French hens,
Two turtle doves, and
A partridge in a pear tree.

The sixth day of Christmas,
My true love sent to me,
Six geese a-laying,
Five gold rings,
Four colly birds,
Three French hens,
Two turtle doves, and
A partridge in a pear tree.

The seventh day of Christmas,
My true love sent to me,
Seven swans a-swimming,
Six geese a-laying,
Five gold rings,
Four colly birds,
Three French hens,
Two turtle doves, and
A partridge in a pear tree.

The eighth day of Christmas,
My true love sent to me,
Eight maids a-milking,
Seven swans a-swimming,
Six geese a-laying,
Five gold rings,
Four colly birds,
Three French hens,
Two turtle doves, and
A partridge in a pear tree.

The ninth day of Christmas,
My true love sent to me,
Nine drummers drumming,
Eight maids a-milking,
Seven swans a-swimming,
Six geese a-laying,
Five gold rings,
Four colly birds,
Three French hens,
Two turtle doves, and
A partridge in a pear tree.

The tenth day of Christmas,
My true love sent to me,
Ten pipers piping,
Nine drummers drumming,
Eight maids a-milking,
Seven swans a-swimming,
Six geese a-laying,
Five gold rings,
Four colly birds,
Three French hens,
Two turtle doves, and
A partridge in a pear tree.

The eleventh day of Christmas,
My true love sent to me,
Eleven ladies dancing,
Ten pipers piping,
Nine drummers drumming,
Eight maids a-milking,
Seven swans a-swimming,
Six geese a-laying,
Five gold rings,
Four colly birds,
Three French hens,
Two turtle doves, and
A partridge in a pear tree.

The twelfth day of Christmas,
My true love sent to me,
Twelve lords a-leaping,
Eleven ladies dancing,
Ten pipers piping,
Nine drummers drumming,
Eight maids a-milking,
Seven swans a-swimming,
Six geese a-laying,
Five gold rings,
Four colly birds,
Three French hens,
Two turtle doves, and
A partridge in a pear tree.

Selector's Notes by Zena Sutherland

The literary history of nursery rhymes grows out of the oral tradition, and there are countless sources: games, plays, prayers, lullabies, counting-out rhymes, riddles, tongue-twisters, alphabet rhymes, and rhymes composed to comment with scorn or praise on real people. Some are taken from folk songs, others from songs by known composers. Some were already old in the reign of Elizabeth I; some are Victorian in origin.

Nursery rhymes and Mother Goose rhymes have become almost synonymous. Several historical figures, including even the Queen of Sheba, have been identified as Mother Goose. Some American scholars have maintained that she was Elizabeth Foster Goose, an American matron whose son-in-law published a collection of rhymes she recalled from her childhood. Supposedly issued in 1719 under the title *Songs for the Nursery; or, Mother Goose's Melodies*, no such publication has ever turned up.

What we do know is that the name "Mother Goose" was first associated with eight folktales recorded by either Charles Perrault or his son Pierre Perrault Darmancour in France around 1697, under the title *Contes de ma Mère l'Oye* (Tales of Mother Goose). But the nursery rhymes that had been sung or told for generations and reached print for the first time in the 1700s became so completely associated with the name "Mother Goose" that most English translations of the Perrault tales now omit the name entirely.

Many of the rhymes were very sophisticated and not originally intended for the young. From the seventeenth century on, there have been those who felt that the rhymes — at least some of them — were unfit for children because of their violence, language, or content, which included such things as murder and racial discrimination. Two of these people were influential writers of the nineteeth century, Sarah Trimmer and Samuel Goodrich. "Too nonsensical," Goodrich protested. To make fun of the genre he composed a silly example of his own, which is how "Higglety, pigglety, pop!" came to be.

The first book designed for children containing some of these verses was *A Little Book for Little Children*. Issued by an author known only as "T.W.," this primer appeared at the beginning of the eighteenth century. It was not until about 1744 that the first substantial nursery rhyme book was printed. *Tommy Thumb's Pretty Song Book* was published in two volumes by Mary Cooper and compiled by an unidentified "N. Lovechild." Copies of Volume 1 no longer exist, and only one edition of the second volume can be found; it is housed in the British Museum.

In 1755 John Newbery (after whom the Newbery Medal is named), published *Nurse Truelove's New-Year's Gift; or, The Book of Books for Children* in London; but it was Newbery's next collection, *Mother Goose's Melody; or, Sonnets for the Cradle* (c. 1765), which may have been edited by Oliver Goldsmith, that became a classic. It is considered the first book to use "Mother Goose" in the title rather than simply "nursery rhymes."

In 1786, Isaiah Thomas produced an American edition of *Mother Goose's Melody*, of which no complete copy is known to exist. Another important title in the accumulating list of nursery rhyme books was *Gammer Gurton's Garland; or, The Nursery Parnassus*, published in London in 1784 by R. Christopher. It was later reissued in expanded editions in 1799 and 1810.

Two major contributions were published in 1805. *The Comic Adventures of Old Mother Hubbard and Her Dog,* written by Sarah Catherine Martin and published by John Harris of London, became an instant and durable favorite. In the same year, *Songs for the Nursery Collected from the Works of the Most Renowned Poets* was published by Benjamin Tabart and Company. Illustrated with hand-colored plates, the book included the first printed versions of such popular rhymes as "Little Miss Muffet" and "One, two, buckle my shoe."

Probably the first truly scholarly investigator of nursery rhymes was James Orchard Halliwell-Phillips. In 1842 he produced his major work, *The Nursery Rhymes of England*, when he was just twenty-two. The contents were gathered from both the oral tradition and bibliographic research. In the next two decades, five expanded editions were published. Subsequent scholars are indebted for many versions and compilations to the wealth of material gathered by Halliwell-Phillips.

Henry Bett's *Nursery Rhymes and Tales: Their Origin and History* was published in 1924. Reflecting the growth of interest in sources, Bett focuses on theories of origin, citing verses as examples, while Halliwell-Phillips focuses largely on the verses themselves.

There is no doubt that Iona and Peter Opie, whose most important work is *The Oxford Dictionary of Nursery Rhymes*, have been both the most untiring scholars and most perspicacious commentators in the field. In this book they state, "We believe that we have assembled here almost everything so far known about nursery rhymes together with a considerable amount of material hitherto unpublished."

Four other reference sources provide varying viewpoints. In *The Real Personages of Mother Goose*, Katherine Elwes Thomas enthusiastically explores sources of the verses in historical events and personages, but much of her material displays a blithe disregard for evidence. In a book that is both scholarly and lively, *Comparative Studies in Nursery Rhymes*, Lina Eckenstein makes comparisons between English verses and their European counterparts. William and Ceil Baring-Gould, in *The Annotated Mother Goose*, provide detailed marginal notes and an extensive bibliography that is arranged chronologically. *An Essay on the Archaeology of Popular English Phrases and Nursery Rhymes*, published in 1834 by John Bellenden Ker, has been described by the Opies as "probably the most extraordinary example of misdirected labour in the history of English letters." Ker claims an early form of Dutch to be the genesis of many of the nursery rhymes.

The narrative poems have most frequently been interpreted with much imagination and little evidence. Different theories of origin for Jack and Jill (who were originally shown as two boys in *Mother Goose's Melody*) hold that they developed from figures in the Norse Edda, or that they were once known as superhuman beings. Thomas, with her usual flair for the dramatic, identifies them as Cardinal Wolsey and Bishop Tarbes, interpreting their journey "up the hill" as their voyage to France to arrange the marriage of Mary Tudor to the French monarch.

"Hey! diddle, diddle," one of the best-known bits of nonsense in the broad spectrum of Mother Goose humor, is known to have appeared as a nursery rhyme in 1765, although parts of it were seen in print in 1569. Katherine Elwes Thomas suggests that the cat was Elizabeth I, but other scholars claim the reference is to Catherine of Aragon or to Catherine the Great.

There *are* some nursery rhymes whose characters are known to have been real people. It is more or less accepted that there really was an incident in which Elizabeth I was startled by a cat in the same way as the queen in "Pussycat, pussycat, where have you been?" And there are several candidates for the role of the merry monarch in "Old King Cole," but the favored one is the King Cole who reigned in Britain in the third century.

The influence of North America is seen in such rhymes as "Hush, little baby," "How much wood would a woodchuck chuck," and "Yankee Doodle." The earliest reference to "Yankee Doodle" appeared in 1768 in the Boston newspaper *Journal of the Times*. Other verses that may have originated in the United States are "There was a young farmer of Leeds," found only in *Gregory Griggs and Other Nursery Rhyme People* and *The Random House Book of Mother Goose*, compiled and illustrated by the late Arnold Lobel. "There was a maid on Scrabble Hill" is found in the Lobel collections as well as in *The Mother Goose Book* compiled and illustrated by Alice and Martin Provensen. When appealed to, Iona Opie did not recognize them, but they have been included here as typical of the form, subject, and humor of so many Mother Goose rhymes.

It is not surprising that fingerplays and other games which stem from the oral tradition should be among the rhymes appearing in the early collections. Rhymes like "This little pig went to market" are still amusing infants today. This verse is referred to in "The Nurse's Song," written about 1728 and published in 1740 in *The Tea-Table Miscellany*. "Pease porridge hot," which is both a clapping game and, in some versions, a riddle ("Spell me that without a P, And a clever scholar you will be") was quoted in part in Newbery's *Mother Goose's Melody*. The game "ring-a-ring o' roses" has been persistently misinterpreted as a reference to plague with its rosy rash, despite the fact that the rhyme first appeared in print in 1881 in Kate Greenaway's *Mother Goose*.

The authorship of most of these rhymes is unknown. Nurse Lovechild, Gammer Gurton, and of course Mother Goose herself remain shadowy figures. Yet, as Harvey Darton in *Children's Books in England: Five Centuries of Social Life* writes, "It is unlikely that any true parentage can ever be found for such dear and homely persons.... It does not matter much. These half-corporeal abstractions appeared in English print, and were admitted to the nursery openly, in the eighteenth century. That is the only indisputable fact."

Illustrator's Notes by Faith Jaques

The nursery rhymes in this collection are set mainly in rural England toward the end of the eighteenth century. Although many of the rhymes originate much earlier and some may even go back to the Middle Ages and before, they had always been handed on by word of mouth, and it was only in the 1780s that books containing collections of nursery rhymes began to be published. This seemed a good reason to set the illustrations in this period. The eighteenth century is an attractive period to illustrate, and everything in the pictures — clothes, houses, domestic detail, gardens — belongs to that time or earlier.

I have based the street scenes on real towns and villages depicted in paintings and engravings, but there are two rhymes set in specific places where it seemed important to show the actual locations. One of them is "I do not like thee, Doctor Fell," which is set in Oxford. Dr. Fell was a much-disliked Dean of Christ Church and I have therefore shown Christ Church in the background. The other rhyme is "Doctor Foster went to Gloucester." I have chosen to illustrate New Inn, a well-known coaching inn which I believe is still standing in the city of Gloucester today.

There is one rhyme, "Hush little baby, don't say a word," which is set in the southern states of the United States. I wanted to make this clear, so I looked for trees which were typical of the area. The picture shows dogwood at the top and cottonwood at the bottom, with magnolia on the left and tulip trees on the right.

Details of decoration, furniture, utensils, and domestic scenes are based on eighteenth-century sources. I have also tried to keep the colors correct — using the soft pinks, lilacs, blues, and greens so distinctive of the Georgian period.

The twenty-four little pictures in "A was an apple pie" each have a different setting and indeed a different apple pie! I have tried to spread the social mix as much as I could; some of the characters lived in splendid eighteenth-century houses and others lived in cottages. The furniture and wallpapers are typical of the period, and in "L longed for it" the beginning of the Chinese influence is seen in the porcelain vase.

"Betty Botter bought some butter" shows a kitchen of the period. The utensils were carefully researched, although Betty herself is a somewhat messy cook! Sugar would be bought as a tall hard cone, mounted on a wooden base. Special cutters were used to cut off a piece at the top which was then flattened back to granular form on a piece of paper with a knife. Flour for daily use was stored in tight-lidded wooden boxes. Cooking pots were made of cast iron, baking dishes of tin or earthenware. Although poor families usually ate off wooden or earthenware platters and bowls, most could afford a china jug, and pewter plates were not uncommon.

In "Three little kittens," there are more utensils and cooking pots; in fact, the rolling pin is very like the ones we use today. The blue-and-white striped dishes still common were also found in eighteenth-century kitchens. Water was heated over the kitchen fire and there was no point in heating up small quantities, so kettles were always very large like the one in "Polly put the kettle on."

"Pease porridge hot" is set in a typical farm kitchen. The pease porridge (a kind of thick soup made from dried or split peas) has been cooked for a very long time in the pot, which is now on the table. The cooking pot would have been suspended over the fire with a chain and hook.

The cake in "Pat-a-cake, pat-a-cake, baker's man" was cooked by the village baker in his oven — a useful arrangement, as villagers who had no oven could have their prepared loaves, pies, and cakes cooked by the baker for a small sum of money.

The domestic animals I have included in the pictures are authentic breeds of the period. The pig was the all-purpose animal kept in villages and it could feed a family for a very long time — no wonder so many rhymes mention them. The dalmatian in "Bow-wow, says the dog" was a fashionable dog for the rich, often trained to run underneath carriages. It was regarded as an elegant accompaniment to one's outfit. The dogs in "Ding, dong, bell" are mongrels, and the one in "This is the house that Jack built" is a whippet — a useful dog in the country for catching rats and rabbits.

Another interesting animal is the woodchuck in the American rhyme " How much wood would a woodchuck chuck." The woodchuck is a northeast American member of the marmot family, and the name comes from the Cree Indian word "wuchak." It can be quite a pest and will eat garden vegetables and flowers, but it is not at all intestested in wood.

One of the pleasures of illustrating the eighteenth century is the richness and variety of the costumes, and indeed the wealth of social history to be found in what people wore.

"Gregory Griggs" is a favorite rhyme and I seized the chance to show twenty-seven different wigs. The little pictures roughly go through the century from about 1730 in the first picture, then show a range of wigs to the end of the century. Although each wig is different, at that time dress changed quite slowly. Clothes were expensive, so even if you were well-to-do you made them last. They were well made, of good quality cloth. Poorer people made their own or bought old secondhand clothes.

Hats were an important part of dress for the period. Men always wore them out-of-doors; women's hair was always covered by a white muslin cap, and poorer women wore a straw hat over the cap. Rich ladies wore large hats over their wigs. In "Three young rats with black felt hats" I have dressed the animals in their best clothes for their walk, all wearing hats except the pigs. I feel that the ducks' "white straw flats" must mean hats. These were an almost flat circle of straw, with hardly any crown; the ribbon was threaded through so that it came down the outside of the brim to give the hat a particular shape.

There were many fashions in shoes for the upper classes. The shoe in "There was an old woman who lived in a shoe" is made of embroidered brocade and typical of the decorative shoes of the period. Men's shoes were generally black with buckles, tassels, or big bows.

The costumes in "The first day of Christmas" are very French. Many sources say that this rhyme was originally a French carol, maybe of the medieval period or even earlier. I have set it in a large estate in rural France. French clothes became very exotic after the Revolution in 1789: the hats were enormous and either worn on top of wigs or on natural hair fuzzed up to make it look bulky. Stripes were fashionable and nearly everything was striped in different widths and different directions. French fashion was based on the sophistication of the town; English fashion was based on country clothes and was much plainer, except for very formal town occasions.

I thoroughly enjoyed researching the origins of the rhymes. For this I must acknowledge the scholarship of Iona and Peter Opie, whose *Oxford Dictionary of Nursery Rhymes* was one of my main sources. Almost every rhyme has a story to tell or can illuminate some aspect of life in the past. There is not the space to expand on this theme here, but the Opies' dictionary is invaluable, and anyone interested in knowing more will see how their comments are the springboard to my illustrations.

Index of First Lines